THE KRELBOYNE PARROT

MALCOLM IN THE MIDDLE™

THE KRELBOYNE PARROT

By Pam Pollack & Meg Belviso

SCHOLASTIC INC.

New York   Toronto   London   Auckland   Sydney
Mexico City   New Delhi   Hong Kong   Buenos Aires

ISBN 0-439-26133-3

12 11 10 9 8 7 6 5 4 3 2 1   1 2 3 5 6/0
Printed in the U.S.A.
First Scholastic printing, September 2001

THE KRELBOYNE PARROT

When I was a kid, like maybe three? I used to watch <u>Mr. Wiffle's Playhouse</u> on TV. I liked the puppets. Hey, I was three. Even Reese watched it when he was three. By the time I started school? I thought it was totally lame and was watching <u>Ninja Robots vs. Skeletrons</u> in the morning like everyone else. So why is my brother Dewey still singing along with Mr. Wiffle and Daisy the Cow Puppet while we're trying to get ready for school?

Reese and I have both talked to him about it. Eventually kids are going to find out. They always find out. And then Mom's going to have to quit her job and home-school him because he won't be able to show his face on the playground. But still there he is every morning listening to Mr. Wiffle's Lesson for Good Boys and Girls. Today's was that if you did something wrong you should:

"Tell your mom or tell your dad
you made a mistake and you've been bad.
You'd better do what you've been taught
'Cause you're gonna get caught,
you're gonna get caught."

How lame is that? But I had to listen to the whole thing because Dewey wouldn't leave for school until it was over. He thinks Daisy the Cow is his friend. And then he wonders why he gets picked last for kick ball.

The worst thing about it? When I finally got him out of the house and dropped him off at his classroom, I realized that stupid song was stuck in my head. As I climbed into the trailer where I have my special genius class, I could hear myself humming, "You're gonna get caught, you're gonna get caught."

CHAPTER ONE

The Krelboyne class is separate from the rest of the school, and I'm a Krelboyne. I don't like to admit it, but I am. It means I'm a genius. The Krelboyne trailer is parked in the playground behind the tetherball court. As I walked into the trailer, I noticed somebody had made a model of the rainforest entirely of tinfoil. There was a giant insect farm sitting on another table that was glassed in so the insects wouldn't escape. And in one corner, taking it all in, was an evil bird beast that watched my every move.

Okay, it's really our class parrot, Hitchcock. He's got black and blue feathers and a beak that looks like it could snap a wrist bone, and probably has. He's got big black talons that make him look like he's wearing brass knuckles, and icy blue eyes. We've had Hitchcock since the beginning of the school year. We've been reading him poetry to see which he likes better, iambic pentameter or free verse. Don't ask. Everyone in the class loves that bird. But not me. I don't like the way his beady eyes follow my every move. I'm convinced that bird doesn't like me.

4

My best friend, Stevie Kenarban, rolled up behind me in his wheelchair. He was wearing a sweater vest with little diamonds on it that made him look like a test pattern. "Hey . . . Malcolm," he said, taking a breath between each word. "Thank . . . God . . . it's . . . Friday."

That took my mind off the parrot. It was almost the weekend, and this Saturday and Sunday? My dad was going to help me, Reese, and Dewey make our own mini-monster-truck for a big rally. We've already got a name picked out — "Truck of Doom." Now we just have to build it and learn how to drive it. How long could that take? As I was imagining myself in the winner's circle with my silver hubcap, something small and hard hit me in the cheek. It was a pellet of birdseed. Hitchcock just spit it at me. It was probably an accident. Birds don't have the brain capacity to plan a seed-spitting, right? But I glared at the parrot anyway.

"Loser!" said Hitchcock, followed by a two-note whistle that was his way of saying "Bite me." We'd tried to teach Hitchcock to recite poetry and speak Latin? But the only things he seemed to retain were insults and swear words.

"I . . . think . . . he . . . likes . . . you," said Stevie. Hitchcock kicked a shower of chewed-up seeds down on Stevie's head. "He . . . did . . . that . . . all . . . the . . . time . . . at . . . my . . . house," Stevie grinned. Hitchcock tipped his water dish over, but Stevie moved his chair back just in time to keep from getting wet.

I couldn't imagine Hitchcock in Stevie's super-neat house with Stevie's super-nervous parents, but every weekend somebody in the class had to take him home. This week was Flor Menash's turn. She's this girl in my class with lopsided pigtails who's allergic to everything — except parrots. Go figure. Next week Hitchcock has to come home with me. Luckily I'd be spending most of my time at the mini-truck rally. What could Hitchcock possibly do to ruin that weekend? Don't answer that.

Hitchcock stared at me all day. During geometry he sharpened his claws and muttered my name over and over. When I came back from lunch? He greeted me with a rude hand gesture. I didn't even know he could twist his claw into that position. Then, when I was giving my oral book report on *Crime and Punishment*, he grabbed the piece of my hair that always sticks up? And yanked me practically off my feet. Finally the teacher had to cut my hair off because the parrot wouldn't let go. He lost interest in it as soon as it wasn't attached to my head. I so hate that parrot.

"Okay, class," the teacher said after she'd disinfected my head, "let's pull our chairs into a circle so we can work on our insect study." She wheeled the bug farm into the center of the room so we could all see the dung beetles and mealworms. They were all from the Amazon. We'd gotten them through a special catalog. I'd voted for the man-eating plant, but we ended up with the bugs. I wouldn't mind bringing a man-eating plant home for the weekend. Maybe it would eat Dewey.

Dabney, Lloyd, and Eraserhead had been studying stingers this semester and got up to give a presentation. "We've made some really exciting discoveries about venom," Eraserhead began. He'd worn a tie to look smarter for the lecture. "Lloyd, would you carefully remove a specimen from the insect farm?"

Lloyd pushed his straight black hair out of his eyes and opened the plastic habitat. Then he used a pair of special tweezers to extract a bug so small none of us could see it anyway. "The *Polophelus Heptamaculatus*," he said proudly, holding up the tweezers.

"You couldn't be more wrong," Dabney said smugly, pushing his glasses up on his round face. "That is a blood-sucking *Trypanosanic Gluteus*."

"Maybe you should put it back," the teacher said nervously.

"Why must you undermine me in front of my colleagues?" Lloyd demanded, spinning to face Dabney and getting red in the face. "Just because I refuse to go along with your insane experiments with crickets?"

Dabney shot back, "You think I'm mad! But my crickets will be my legacy!"

Eraserhead stepped between them. "Okay, put the

specimen back. You're too hysterical to handle a creature of the jungle."

"I don't think they're handling anything," another voice said. Everybody turned around. It was Martin Stephens, casually flipping a pencil through his fingers. "The insect, whatever it is, has escaped and stung Flor."

Now everybody turned to Flor, whose face was three times the size it was five minutes ago and swelling before our eyes. She looked a little like Humpty Dumpty with lopsided pigtails. And these weird red spots on her arms. Flor seemed like she was trying to yell? But she could only squeak through her nose.

"She's gonna blow!" yelled Dabney, flattening himself against the wall in horror. "Now, look what you've done!"

"I told you it was a *Polophelus Heptamaculatus*," said Lloyd, starting to cry.

I have to admit, I was impressed. She was swelling even more than Dad did the time he was bitten by a ladybug. It took all four of us to roll him back to the car when that happened. Who ever heard of somebody being allergic to ladybugs? Only my dad as far as I know.

The teacher ran to her desk and started flipping through the emergency manual? Like there was going to be something in there about what to do if you got bitten by a rare bug from the Amazon jungle.

By this time the class was in a panic. Stevie was trying to get away from the bugs, but his wheels were just spinning in place? He'd forgotten to take the brake off. Eraserhead was sure he was covered in invisible bugs and started ripping off his clothes. Lloyd was crying "Forgive me, Flor!" over and over, while Dabney yelled "I'm a disgrace to the scientific community." Martin was looking up "mass hysteria" in his psychology book.

Obviously, I was going to have to take care of this. I jumped up and helped Flor out of her chair. Even at her maximum density, Flor was much easier to move than my dad. Plus, she wasn't howling "Lois! Lois!" like my dad had been that day. I pulled Flor out of the trailer to the nurse. Another minute and her head wouldn't have fit through the door.

"Thanks, Malcolm," Flor wheezed as I walked her past the tetherball. I couldn't see her mouth, her cheeks were so big. "I guess you'll have to take care of Hitchcock this weekend."

For a second? I almost wished it was me that got stung by that bug. Not that I want to look like an overripe grapefruit, but it couldn't be that much worse than a whole weekend with Hitchcock. But there was nothing I could do. I walked with Flor into the nurse's office. I wish I could describe the look on the nurse's face when she saw us coming? One genius kid guiding an egg with legs over the playground. Bet she wasn't expecting that.

After I dropped Flor off, I dragged my feet back into the trailer. Inside, I glanced up at my weekend houseguest.

Hitchcock looked me right in the eye, slowly raised his cuttlebone to his beak, and snapped it in two.

I think he was imagining it was me.

CHAPTER TWO

Stevie offered to help me get Hitchcock back to my house. I set the cage on Stevie's lap and pushed his wheelchair from behind. I'd put the cover over the cage because I didn't like the idea of that bird knowing the way to my house. Can't be too careful. Parrots have a killer homing instinct.

"Are you sure your parents won't let you come to the mini-monster-truck rally?" I asked him. It seemed so wrong that "Wheels" Kenarban wasn't allowed to go to a truck rally.

"My . . . mom . . . says . . . the . . . fumes . . . make . . . you . . . stupid," Stevie said with a shrug.

"No they don't," I said. "My brother Reese is always going to truck rallies and he's not stupid. Oh wait, yes he is. Point taken."

"Stupid," Hitchcock repeated under the cover. Stevie jumped in his chair. For a second I wondered if he was afraid of Hitchcock. Not that I'm afraid of Hitchcock. He's just a bird. I'm a genius human. Anyway, then Stevie laughed.

"You . . . got . . . me," Stevie said to the cage. I kind of wished Stevie would just forget he had this big cage on his lap and take it home. Then I just wouldn't answer the phone all weekend. He'd be stuck taking care of the bird instead of me. But when we got to my house? He practically shoved the cage into my hands. Then he sped down the street like he had a motor on his wheelchair. I was left standing there in front of our yard. The grass was growing in crooked ever since Reese and I got into a fight with the lawnmower.

I got a better grip on the heavy cage and turned toward the house. Okay, so I had to take care of a bigmouthed bird for the weekend. It was only sixty-four hours and twenty-seven minutes until I could give him back. What could happen in that amount of time?

The front door opened and Dewey came out banging a coffee can. It was hanging from his neck by a strap he'd attached to the can by punching holes in the top and bottom. You'd think he would use an empty coffee can? But instead he was trailing the grounds behind him wherever he went. As he marched by me down the sidewalk, he drummed and sang, "You'd better do what you've been taught 'cause you're gonna get caught, you're gonna get caught."

He really needs to start watching *Skeletrons*.

When I dragged the heavy cage into the house, I ran into Mom dragging an even heavier vacuum cleaner. She must have brought it from the Lucky

Aid store where she works. Her brown laser eyes immediately went to the big, covered thing in my hand.

"What's that?" she asked, pointing to the cage.

"It's my class parrot," I said. "I was supposed to get him next weekend but Flor Menash got bitten by a *Polophelus Heptamaculatus* and —"

"Well, it better not make a mess," Mom said. "And if it does you better clean it up before I see it."

I looked down and saw a trail of coffee grounds. It led from our room down the hall, through the living room, three times around the kitchen, and then out the front door. No wonder Mom was mad. She picked up the vacuum hose and waved the sucker in my face. "This is the strongest vacuum that's legal in this state," she said. "I pleaded with them at work to let me take it home for the weekend and clean up after you boys. Come on."

Mom led me down the hall into the bedroom I shared with my brothers. All except one. Through a series of misunderstandings my brother Francis got sent away to military school. It was so unfair. Francis always had bad luck. Right now he was in trouble at school so we weren't sure he could come home for the rally. Luckily Mom didn't know about it. I knew Francis would find a way out. He never gets punished for anything. I wish he still lived here. Anyway, since Francis had left, Reese, Dewey, and I kept the room pretty messy between us.

"Look at this place," Mom said, opening the door.

I looked. Jelly handprint on the wall next to Dewey's bed. Reese's underwear hanging from the lamp. Beds unmade. Pile of car magazines. G.I. Joe with one leg (we'd had to amputate). One glass full of something that used to be milk. Everything seemed to be in order.

"What's the matter?" I asked Mom.

Mom's eyes rolled up to the ceiling and back. "Were you raised by wolves?" she asked.

"No, we were raised by —"

"Forget it," Mom said. "This place is a sty. A disaster area. A toxic dump. A pig lagoon! Honestly, your father and I work hard to make you a nice home and everything you boys touch turns to garbage."

She took a breath and it seemed like she'd finished talking. "So do you want me to clean my room?" I asked.

Mom leaned down close to me and looked me right in the eye. "I want this room scrubbed, polished, and buffed. I want your clean clothes put in the drawers. I want your dirty clothes put in the laundry. I want everything picked up off the floor. Then I'm going to give you this vacuum and you're going to suck every subatomic particle of dirt off this rug. You got it?"

I was too scared to speak so I just nodded.

"Good." Mom went back into the living room. A second later I heard the roar of the super-vacuum as she attacked the trail of coffee grounds. I sighed and cleaned off a place on my desk for the birdcage. Then I started picking things up. It wasn't fair. First I had to take care of this awful bird and then I had to touch Reese's underwear. Okay, I wasn't going to let this bird ruin my whole weekend. Nobody could ruin a whole weekend except Mom. And Hitchcock was no Mom.

"Everything you touch turns to garbage!"

I spun around, expecting to see Mom in the door-way. "I'm cleaning like you told me to . . ." I began. Nobody was there. I looked at Hitchcock's cage. It couldn't be. "Everything you touch turns to garbage!" he screamed from under the cover.

Oh my God. There are two of them now. The bird had been here five minutes and already it was mim-icking my mom yelling at me.

"Were you raised by wolves?" Hitchcock said. Twelve times in a row.

This was too much. I marched over to the cage and ripped the cover off. Hitchcock blinked in the sud-den daylight. Then he made a rude noise with his beak.

"Listen," I said, pointing my finger at his face. "I am so much higher than you are on the food chain. You better watch out."

Hitchcock snapped at my finger but I pulled it away just in time. I really meant it. That bird had better watch out. I grabbed Reese's underwear off the lamp, went over to the wall, and cleaned off the jelly handprint with it. As I tossed the underwear into the hamper, I heard a splat and turned around. Where the handprint had been there was now a greenish brown smudge. I stared at the cage. What's up with that? How did Hitchcock get bird poop halfway across the room?

He must have known I was wondering? Because he demonstrated for me. He picked up a pile of bird sludge in his claw and winged it at me. If I hadn't ducked? It would have got me right in the eye. He was going to have to be faster than that if he wanted to throw poop at me. In my family you learn to duck at an early age.

I started cleaning as fast as possible. The faster I cleaned, the faster I could get away from the bird. While I cleaned, Hitchcock yelled at me — in my mom's voice! "Sty! Disaster area! Toxic dump! PIG LAGOON!" Even though I knew it wasn't really my mom's voice? It still made me clean faster. If I didn't get out of this room soon I was going to cement his beak shut with airplane glue. Finally I was finished. Then I was wet. How did that happen?

Oh, now I see. Hitchcock was sitting in his water dish furiously flapping his wings so that water sprayed all over. When he was done, I had to refill his water dish. He emptied three of them before he got bored.

I put my face close to the cage and looked the parrot in the eye. "Listen, you little . . ."

The bedroom door opened and Mom hauled in the vacuum. I stood up straight. I tried to look innocent — like I wasn't just threatening the bird. Mom glanced at my now-clean room. "Pretty good," she said. Then she noticed the puddles. "Except for pouring water on everything. Malcolm, what were you thinking?"

"It wasn't me," I said. "It was —"

Mom put the vacuum nozzle into my hand. "Here's how you work it," she said. She pointed to a dial on the side of the vacuum. "There're five settings. Don't ever go higher than three. You'll suck the boards right out of the floor. That's how powerful it is. Don't go near anything you ever want to see again. Keep your hands and feet away from the nozzle. Don't put it in your mouth."

Reese had been seven years old when that happened? And he still wasn't allowed to use the vacuum. But he could touch his nose with his tongue now and he couldn't do that before. So it was worth it.

"You're the only one I trust with this, Malcolm," said Mom. "Don't let me down."

Mom went into the kitchen to start dinner, and I looked at the vacuum. It really was cool. It was too bad this kind of technology was wasted on something to clean with. It would make an excellent toy. I would buy one.

I turned the dial up to three and felt a kick in the

nozzle as the super-sucking power started. Then I started vacuuming. I don't know what I was picking up with it, but it turns out our bedroom rug is yellow. Reese and Dewey would really be surprised that it wasn't the grayish brown it always had been. I accidentally sucked up G.I. Joe's leg. It had rolled under the radiator after we operated. It was okay. Joe managed just fine on the wooden leg we'd made. And he looked a lot cooler. Then I accidentally sucked up Dewey's baby teeth. Then I sucked up Reese's black belt from karate. I did that on purpose because he didn't really earn his black belt. He just beat up the kid that did.

When I was finished, the room was totally clean. I couldn't wait for Mom to see it. She might even make red-hot sundaes for dessert. I looked over the room one more time. This time I noticed there was a crayon sticking out from under Dewey's mattress. I think it was periwinkle. I bent down and pulled it out. When I turned back around, the entire room was covered in birdseed. The rug was crunchy. I locked eyes with Hitchcock. Then I looked at his claw. He was flipping me off again.

Once when I was in first grade? I collected box tops from Sugar Bomb cereal for ten months. I only needed one more to get the remote-controlled atomic rocket. I dreamed about that rocket for ten months. The day I cut out my last box top, Reese traded my collection to some kid for X-ray glasses. I mean, how could he even think they would work? I thought I was angry then. I didn't know the meaning of the word. Now I was angry.

I wanted to get that parrot. Pluck out his feathers. Punch him in the beak. Imitate *his* mother until he went insane. But I couldn't do any of that. I was the homo sapien. I had to be the bigger person.

I grabbed the vacuum hose and slung it over my shoulder. *Stupid bird!* I thought.

"Stupid Malcolm!" said Hitchcock.

He did *not* just say that.

I dropped down on my knees and spun the dial. I jerked it so hard it went right past three and landed on five. The hose sprang to life, pulling me backward. I heard a strange sound. Something like "Gwaaaak!" followed by a *shoomp!* The nozzle bucked. Like a snake trying to swallow a bowling ball? For a second there was a strange lump in the vacuum tube and then it was gone. I hoped I hadn't just sucked up my autographed baseball. I turned off the vacuum and looked over my shoulder. The baseball was safe — that was a relief. I waited for Hitchcock to start insulting me again.

He wasn't there. The cage was empty. Two of the bars were bent outwards almost in the shape of a parrot. Two blue feathers drifted to the floor below it. Slowly I picked up the vacuum hose and looked inside. Half of a third blue feather was stuck in the nozzle.

I thought about that strange lump traveling down the vacuum tube. And that "Gwaaaak!" that sounded sort of like a parrot cursing me out for the last time right before he kicked the bucket. It was kind of echoing in my head.

The parrot was no more.

CHAPTER THREE

I didn't mean it. I didn't mean to get rid of Hitch-cock. I know everybody thinks I did. Or they will think it once they find out. And they will find out. They always find out.

I imagined myself coming into school on Monday with the empty cage. "Where's the bird, Malcolm?" everyone would ask.

"H-h-he had an accident," I'd stammer, starting to sweat.

Lloyd would jump up on his chair and point his finger at me. "J'accuse!" That means he's accusing me in French.

"We knew you hated that bird, Malcolm," Eraserhead would say, shaking his head. "But we never thought you'd go this far."

Had the whole class noticed how when I read to Hitchcock I always chose poems the teacher said were "downers"?

"He probably sabotaged our venom presentation," Dabney would say, lifting up his glasses and squinting at me. I hated it when he did that. "He got

Flor out of the way so there would be nothing to stop his maniacal plan to rub out the parrot!"

Okay, that was totally unfair.

Suddenly the door would bang open and Flor would roll in like a beachball. "You did it," she'd cry. "You did it!"

The rest of the class would join in, crowding around me and singing "You did it, you did it."

Stevie would say, "You . . . did . . . it." Even Stevie was against me.

Suddenly, in my mind, I was on stage in front of the whole school. I was put in the stocks like a criminal in Colonial America. Everyone was throwing bird-seed at me while I kept screaming, "I didn't mean it! I really didn't!"

I shook my head to get the awful fantasy out of it.

Man, that was weird. Okay, I'm totally letting my imagination get away from me. Stocks? My school doesn't have stocks. The kindergarten teacher has an "uncooperative chair," but that's about it.

"Malcolm?" my mom called from the living room. "Are you almost finished with the vacuum?"

Oh no. Mom. "Just a minute," I called back. I started vacuuming up the seeds as fast as I could. The super-sucker didn't seem to be sucking things up the way it had before. Maybe I was just jumpy. All I knew was that I couldn't get the evidence up fast enough.

As I vacuumed, I imagined telling my family what I'd done to Hitchcock.

"Are you sure you didn't just misplace the parrot, son?" my dad would ask.

"Hal, he didn't misplace it, he bumped it off!" Mom would yell. "Your son's the Terminator!"

"No," I would try to explain. "It wasn't like that."

"Is Malcolm going to jail?" Dewey would ask.

"No," Mom would say. "And he's not going to any mini-monster-truck rally either!"

I turned off the vacuum, sat down on the floor, and let my head fall into my hands, still gripping the murder weapon — I mean the vacuum tube! Who was I kidding? I wasn't going to any mini-monster-truck rally. Murderers don't get to go to mini-monster-truck rallies. I couldn't believe it. Even in death that parrot was ruining everything. There was no way I was missing that rally. I just had to figure out what to do.

I wished Francis was here. He would know what to do. Francis knew all about guilt and how to make it go away. When you don't feel guilty you can think better. Like the time I was in kindergarten? My teacher was wearing a new coat. It was really ugly but she must have liked it a lot. She hardly ever took it off, even when she went to the bathroom. Well, she took it off one day, during finger painting. I accidentally spilled brown paint on it. And yellow. And some green splatters. And it wasn't really an accident. When she came back in the room, she asked who did it. I hid my fingers under the desk and pretended I was coloring with crayons that day. No one else had seen me do it.

I didn't get caught? But I felt really bad about it. Every time I saw her come in wearing her old coat I felt worse. But Francis said, "Listen Malcolm. You said the coat was ugly, right? And the whole class thought it was ugly?"

"We called it the Dead Muppet Coat," I said.

"Right," said Francis. "So in a way, you did her a favor. You saved her from her own poor fashion taste."

See how cool Francis is? He always makes everything seem better. I wish he was here now, but he's not.

Okay, so here are my options. I can let Mom find out what happened on her own — she always does — and get in trouble. Or I could confess. We hardly ever confessed. Maybe just the novelty of it would get me points. I decided to confess to Mom and get it over with. Just as I stood up, the door banged open and Reese came in, bouncing a basketball. The basketball froze in his hand. He could sense something was wrong. I saw his eyes move from the empty cage to the vacuum cleaner tube in my hand with feathers beside it. Back to the cage. Back to the vacuum. Back to the cage.

He didn't get it.

"Dude, hand over the vacuum," he said. "I want to see if I can suck the basketball into it."

That would be neat. Wait. No it wouldn't.

"No," I said. Suddenly the thought of seeing how many things we could suck into the vacuum seemed a little sick.

"Hey, you got to clean the whole room with it. It's my turn."

I held onto the vacuum and shook my head. For a second I could swear I heard something whisper "Malcolm" from deep inside the tube. I mean, I didn't *really* hear it. I just thought I did. That's called auditory hallucination. I'm sure it's really common. "Stay away from it!" I cried.

"What's your problem?" asked Reese. "Did you stick it in your mouth?"

When Reese is stupid enough to do something? He thinks everyone's stupid enough to do it. "No," I said. "I just don't want you to break it. It's already sounding funny."

Reese thought for a long moment. Then he pointed his finger at me. "You put something in there," he said triumphantly. "Mom is so going to flip when she finds out you broke the super-sucker."

"It's not broken," I snapped. "See?" I switched the vacuum on and off quickly.

"So what did you do?" Reese pressed. "I know you did something. There's fear in your eyes. I can sense fear." Suddenly Reese leaped at me, landing on his knees right in front of me. He made sort of kung-fu movements (but really just Reese-imitating-kung-fu-guys-on-TV) with his hands all around my face. Normally it would just be annoying? But now it reminded me of Hitchcock's flapping wings. Suddenly I really wanted to see one of his rude claw gestures again.

"Whaaaaa," Reese wailed, still playing the kung-fu master. "There is no escape," he said.

Like I really needed this now when I was about to be banned from the monster truck rally.

"Reese, leave me alone," I said.

"Little muskrat who reeks of guilt will soon be smelled by the tiger," Reese said. "I am the tiger."

I hate it when Reese goes all *Crouching Tiger* on me. Especially now, because I did reek of guilt. I could smell it myself.

"You look like an idiot," I told him. Reese didn't care.

"The tiger has legs like steel springs," he went on. "The tiger has teeth like knives."

"The tiger has breath like meatball hoagie," I said. He was going to keep breathing in my face until I talked. I could feel sweat on my upper lip. I was about to crack. Anything to get away from Reese.

"The tiger has stripes like —"

Then I opened my mouth and it just came out. "I knocked off the parrot!" I shouted.

Reese blinked at me, confused. "What?"

"My class parrot," I babbled. "I took him home for the weekend and he threw seeds all over and I tried to vacuum them up, but I put the vacuum on five. I meant to put it on three. The parrot . . . the parrot's gone."

"You mean he's . . . in here?" Reese asked, pointing to the vacuum. I nodded. "Is he stuck?"

"Reese," I said. "He's . . . he's deceased. We're talking about an ex-parrot."

"Cool!" said Reese, grabbing the vacuum and starting to open it. "Let's do an autopsy!"

Okay, normally? I would be up for that. Death by vacuum doesn't happen every day. I could win the science fair. Wait! What was *I* saying? I couldn't win the science fair by murdering a parrot. There's probably a rule about that.

"Reese, we can't do an autopsy," I said. "I'm going to tell Mom what happened. If I'm lucky she'll let me go to the rally before she grounds me for life. Everybody'll find out anyway. I'm supposed to bring the parrot back to class on Monday."

"Why don't you just replace it?" Reese said.

"What?" Now I was confused.

"Duh," said Reese. "Replace him. That's what they always do on TV when a bird gets lost or something.

Just go to the pet store and get another one. No one will be able to tell the difference. Not even a Krelboyne. All birds look alike."

As stupid as that sounded? It just might work. And hadn't I already suffered enough for Hitchcock? There was only one thing wrong with the plan. It was Reese's. I shook my head. "No. Absolutely not. Something bad will happen. It'll backfire somehow. Your plans always do."

"You got a better one?"

Before I could come up with anything else, Dewey came in with his empty coffee can. He was still singing, "You're gonna get caught, you're gonna get caught." I quickly threw the cover back over the cage. "What's in there?" asked Dewey.

I told him as briefly as possible about Hitchcock. "But he's resting," I said. "He's just had a long squawk. So you can't disturb him."

Dewey tried to peer under the cover and into the cage.

"If you get too close," I added, "he'll peck your eyes out."

If Hitchcock were still alive? That would have been the truth.

"C'mon," I said. "It's time for dinner."

Dewey left, not taking his eyes off the cage until he was out the door.

That was easier than I thought. Hiding this was going to be no problem. All I had to do was replace the

bird and nobody got hurt. Well, nobody else would
get hurt.

I looked at Reese, my new partner in crime. He was
staring down at his feet.

"Hey," said Reese. "Since when is this rug yellow?"

You know, the clock in our room makes a really loud ticking sound? You don't notice it unless you're lying awake thinking how you're going to replace a dead parrot in the morning.

I kept going over the plan so I'd get it right. Wake up early. Go to the mall. Don't let the cage out of my sight. Sell my most valuable possession. Use the money to buy another Hitchcock. It was the perfect plan.

Reese wasn't thinking about the plan. Nobody could snore that loudly and think. Dewey was having his evil jack-in-the-box dream. I could tell because he was tossing and turning and mumbling "Pop Goes the Weasel" every five minutes.

Still sleeping, Reese got out of bed and bopped Dewey over the head with his pillow. Still sleeping, Dewey whined, "I'm telling!" and then rolled over. As

Reese collapsed back into his own bed, I wondered how many fights Reese and I had had while we were sleeping.

I turned over and stared at the silent cage on my desk. It was the loudest silence ever.

CHAPTER FOUR

Finally it was morning. I stayed close to the cage at all times. I knew if he got the chance? Dewey would look under the cover.

"Is Hitchcock awake?" Dewey asked me as he came out of the bathroom in his Daisy the Cow Puppet pajamas. I can't believe Mom lets him wear those things. I can't believe they even make them in his size. Somebody should start a support group for kids wearing cartoon characters they were too old for.

"No," I said. "He's not a morning person. He hates mornings. If you talk to him in the morning? He'll peck your eyes out."

Dewey's big blue eyes got wide and he tried to look in the cage again.

"Go away, you little weirdo!" I screeched in my best Hitchcock voice. I knew that ventriloquist kit I bought when I was eight would come in handy some day.

Dewey jumped back from the cage. "Daisy the Cow Puppet says it's not nice to peck people's eyes out," he said.

I wondered if Daisy had a song about that. Without trying to, I made one up in my head:

*"Pecking out eyes is very mean
The meanest I have ever seen
Biting ears is rotten too
You wouldn't like it if it happened to you."*

Okay, now I was really losing it. I was making up stupid songs for TV puppets. "Dewey, go to breakfast," I said.

Dewey sighed and went out humming, "You're gonna get caught, you're gonna get caught."

As soon as he was gone? I grabbed a pair of pliers and bent the bars back the way they were before Hitchcock went speeding through them. Then I quickly got dressed and went into the kitchen. The plans for Truck of Doom were lying out on the counter next to a list of stuff to get from the auto supply store at the mall.

"Dewey, get your fork out of the toaster," Mom said as I sat down. "Malcolm, you look terrible. Are you coming down with something?"

"Muskrat guilt," Reese said under his breath so only I could hear. I glared at him. Reese picked up a pat of butter and held it in front of his mouth, holding his lips in a circle. Then he sucked loudly and the butter flew into his mouth with a smaller version of the same *shoomp* that Hitchcock had made in the vacuum. I pushed away my pancakes. I wasn't hungry anymore. I'd feel better once we replaced the parrot.

"Dad," Reese said, cramming a whole microwave

pancake into his mouth. "Malcolm and I have to go the pet store at the mall."

Dad looked confused. He always looks confused. He was wearing a black T-shirt with a skull driving a flaming race car on it. It said BORN TO BURN RUBBER and there were smoking tire tracks across his stomach. He always wore that shirt when we went to the auto supply store. "Reese, we discussed this," he said. "According to the mini-truck driver's oath, we can't have any live projectile missiles on Truck of Doom. Have we learned nothing from the flying gerbil fiasco? Do you want to get disqualified?"

"I thought they were bats," mumbled Reese, stabbing a pancake with his fork.

"It's not for Truck of Doom, Dad," I explained. He was taking us all to the mall after breakfast to get the parts we still needed to build our monster machine.

We had some parts already. Mom had brought home some empty wooden wine crates that said HAUT BRION on the side. She got them from Chanceux Assiste, the French restaurant across the parking lot from the Lucky Aid. Reese went to the golf course and came back with some wheels from the golf carts. He didn't tell us exactly how he got them. And Stevie was really mad when his parents wouldn't let him come to the rally? So he offered the use of their new lawnmower's engine for Truck of Doom. They'd probably be happy about it when we won.

"I need to get some food for my class parrot at the mall," I told Dad.

"Just make sure that food doesn't end up on my rugs," Mom said. "From either end of the bird."

"There was a kid in my class," said Dewey. "He was really smart. And then one day . . . it turned out . . . he was a parrot."

"No he wasn't," said Reese.

"That's nice, son," said Dad.

I didn't say anything. I was staring at the super-sucker sitting in the corner of the kitchen. It was weird seeing it just sitting there after what happened yesterday.

"Is this a vacuum I see before me?" I mumbled.

"What?"

I snapped out of it. My whole family was looking at me strangely. "I mean, when are you bringing that thing back?" I asked. My voice was kind of shaky for some reason. It was probably from hunger, so I ate a pancake.

"Today," Mom said. "Your dad's dropping me off at work when he takes you kids to the mall. So hurry up and eat."

Nobody ever had to tell us to hurry up and eat. In five minutes the food was gone and the table was a mess. "Let's ride," said Dad.

"I don't want to sit in the middle!" Dewey wailed as we crammed into the car.

"Too bad," Reese said, shoving him over.

I climbed into the car and put the cage on my lap. I wrapped my arms around it like it might escape or something.

"Malcolm, why are you bringing that bird to the mall?" Mom said, pointing to it.

"If you get too close he'll peck your eyes out," Dewey informed her.

"Not unless he wants to end up plucked and fried for dinner," Mom answered. "Malcolm, what's with the birdcage?"

"He has to come with us," I improvised. "If he doesn't pick the food out himself he won't eat it."

Mom snorted. "That's something I never have to worry about with you guys."

I kept my arms wrapped around the cage. Dewey kept trying to slide his fingers through the bars. If Hitchcock had really been in there? Dewey would have had nothing but bloody stumps by the time we got to the mall.

"Okay," I told Dad when we got out of the car. "Reese and I will go to the pet store and meet you at Greased Lightnin'." That's the auto supply store.

Before we went to the pet store? We had to stop off at the comic book store. For the first time in my life, I didn't want to go in there. In order to buy a new parrot? I was going to have to sell my special edition *Youngblood #27*. It was a limited edition. The one where Kodiak meets his father and then War Wolf kills him. I would rather have sold one of my toes.

"Are you crazy?" asked the bald girl with the nose ring behind the counter when she saw what I was selling.

"Yeah," I mumbled. "I really need the money."

She called her boss over. He was bald, too, with a beard and glasses. He was wearing a T-shirt that said "Criminals are a superstitious, cowardly lot." — Bruce Wayne.

It was a bad sign that he was wearing that T-shirt. I knocked on the wooden shelf behind me and almost ran out of the store. Then I realized I was being superstitious and cowardly. Bruce Wayne was right. As usual.

The comic book guy shook his head sadly as I turned over my comic. "Live long and prosper," he said. I said I would try.

When I came out of the store, even Reese looked sympathetic. "You had to do it, Muskrat," he said. "Tiger is pleased."

I dragged the birdcage into La Cage Aux Folles. It was a pet store that specialized in exotic birds with beautiful plumage. There were cages and cages of weird-looking birds with feathers sticking up out of their heads? And they were making the biggest racket I've ever heard. It was worse than our house.

"I need to buy a parrot," I told the guy at the counter. He had his hair puffed up and falling over his eyes so he looked like a bird himself. "He has to

be blue with big claws and a beak like . . . like that!"
I pointed to a cage with a parrot inside that looked
just like Hitchcock!

The salesman followed my finger. "Remarkable
bird, the Norwegian Blue," he said as he went over
to it. "And very popular around here." He tapped on
the cage. "Hello, Mr. Polly Parrot," he said brightly.

"Bite me," the bird said.

"He's perfect!" I cried. "We'll take him. Put him in
the cage."

As the salesman put my new parrot into the cage, I
felt somebody watching me. I turned around but
there was no one there except more birds. Lots of
birds. Watching me. Like they knew.

CHAPTER FIVE

"I am going to take such good care of you," I said to my new parrot, Hitchcock 2. "Just stay alive, whatever may occur."

"Dude, get off your knees, you're embarrassing me," Reese said, pulling me up from the floor. "Let's go meet Dad."

I hurried along behind him, trying to keep the cage steady, but it kept banging into my knees.

"Watch it, spaz," the parrot squawked. It was music to my ears. I couldn't believe it, but Reese's plan was working like a charm. I'd practically forgotten that this wasn't the same parrot.

"I'm so not going to get caught," I said to Reese. "I'll never doubt you again. You're a genius."

"The kind of genius I am they don't teach in school," Reese said. "I keep trying to tell Mom that."

He had a point. Even in the Krelboyne class they didn't teach parrot replacement. No way Mom would understand.

When we got to Greased Lightnin', Dad and Dewey were trying out the different replacement seat covers. I put Hitchcock's cage on the counter next to a box of novelty key chains that looked like silver bolts of lightning. There was also a box of souvenir pens that, when you tipped them, showed two cars drag racing. "Now you be a good parrot, Hitchcock. And I'll give you a nice fresh cuttlefish when we get home." I shook the bag holding the cuttlefish I bought at La Cage Aux Folles in front of the cage.

Hitchcock kicked a pile of birdseed in my face. It tasted salty.

"Hey boys, take a look at these," my dad called from in front of a wall of decals. We could put some on Truck of Doom when it's finished. Reese and I both grabbed for the same pair of fuzzy dice.

"Is Hitchcock awake, Malcolm?" asked Dewey. "Can he talk now?"

I was really happy to be able to tell him that Hitchcock was, finally, awake. "Yeah," I said. "When he saw all the spark plugs in here he perked right up."

Dewey ran over to Hitchcock's cage. I figured a talking bird would keep him occupied for at least fifteen minutes.

I grabbed the fuzzy dice from Reese. "Now get that sticker with the rattlesnake on it."

Reese shook his head and went for the Screaming Eagle. It said "Mess with the best, die with the rest" on it. I had to admit it was a pretty cool slogan. But it was also a bird. I had bad luck with birds. Enough with the birds.

"Reese, get the rattlesnake," I said. "Truck of Doom

doesn't fly, it shoots across the ground like a deadly snake and then strikes its enemies with terrifying speed." I should know. I designed it.

"Will you excuse us, Dad?" Reese said in a fake polite voice. He led me over to the corner. "Malcolm, who just saved your butt with that parrot thing?"

I opened my mouth, but there was nothing I could say. Reese did.

"And who could get your butt grounded if he told Mom?"

I gritted my teeth and tried to figure a way out. Reese had me trapped like a . . . muskrat. "Get the eagle," I muttered. I'd let him have this one. But that was it.

"Thank you, Malcolm," Reese said with a smirk. "This arrangement is going to work out very well."

That's what you think, I thought. Reese went back to the stickers and I considered my options. I didn't really have any. Reese and the parrot were going to be on my back the entire weekend. Could I stand it till Monday? If it meant going to the mini-monster-truck rally, I could.

I headed back to Reese, who had just picked out the color bandana he wanted us all to wear during the rally: tiger stripe. Dad wanted urban camouflage.

"Which do you like, Malcolm?" said Dad. He gave a look that meant *Side with me and I'll take you to an R-rated movie.*

"I like the urban . . ." I began.

Reese cleared his throat.

I tried to ignore him. "I like the ur . . ."

Reese squawked softly. Then he whistled like a parrot. I glared at him. I'd just sold my comic book for this plan. I wasn't going to blow it now.

"Tiger stripe," I mumbled.

"Fine Malcolm, whatever you want," Dad pouted. "Don't worry about letting me down. Be your own man." He turned away to check out the socket sets.

"Oh, by the way," said Reese. "When we fill out the entry form on Truck of Doom, we should put my name down as the designer."

Now I was more angry than I was when Reese traded my box tops for fake X-ray glasses. If I had a vacuum I would definitely have sucked Reese into it.

"Forget it, Reese," I yelled. "I designed Truck of Doom. Remember? I'm the genius."

"*I'm* the genius," said Reese. "Remember?"

Parrot or no parrot, this was going too far. I got ready to launch myself at him. Before I could? Something small and hard landed on my head. "Ow!" I said, looking up. A lightning bolt key chain landed at my feet. Several more followed it.

"Hey!" Reese yelled, covering his head and ducking for cover. "What is this?"

I looked up as a shower of fuses rained down. It was Hitchcock 2. He was flying around picking things up and bombing everyone in the store with them, whistling and screeching at the top of his lungs. He swooped down over a basket of batteries, grabbed a clawful, and then hurled them at the customers, making a sound like a bomber plane.

"Dear God, what is it?" Dad screamed.

"Save yourselves," a man called to his children. They ran out of the store with their coats over their heads. Hitchcock lobbed some air fresheners after them.

"Who let that parrot out?" I shouted. I crawled on the floor toward where I'd left the cage. A big guy in overalls almost stepped on my hand. Suddenly there was a flood of sticky oil spilling across the floor. Hitchcock 2 had overturned an open can of brake fluid on the counter. He followed it with a quick radiator coolant spill.

All the people who were running and screaming were now running and sliding and screaming.

Hitchcock 2 picked up an aerosol can of florescent pink paint. With his claw on the button, he started spraying all the walls. I don't know what he was writing, but knowing Hitchcock 2, it was probably some rude parrot graffiti.

"Malcolm," cried Dad. "In the name of all that is good and pure, DO SOMETHING!"

I looked back and saw Reese cowering in the corner. "Oh my God, he's got the souvenir pens!" he gasped as a hail of them hit the puddles, splashing oil everywhere.

I put my head down and crawled forward until I reached a dirty pair of sneakers attached to a dirty pair of jeans and a striped T-shirt. Dewey smiled down at me, sucking a Greased Lightnin' souvenir lollipop.

"Why did you let him out?" I asked. I don't know why I ask Dewey these questions? I just had to know.

"Hitchcock wanted to shop too," said Dewey. "He'll come back when he's finished. He promised. He's my friend."

Sure enough, Hitchcock flew back into his cage and tucked his head under his wing. Right after he set off some emergency flares.

When the sparks disappeared and everyone realized the terror was over, they made a run for the door.

"Don't go," the owner of the store called after them. "Half price on gas additives to anyone who continues to shop."

One guy in a T-shirt looked tempted but his friend in a baseball cap that said *NO FEAR* dragged him out. "Let's get out of here. Who knows when Rodan the flying monster will attack again?"

I think somebody needed to buy a new baseball cap.

Soon it was just us and the store owner. Somehow I didn't think we were going to get the half off on gas additives.

"Get out!" he said. "If you ever come near this store again I'm calling the police."

That's when it got embarrassing. Dad started to

cry. He told the guy how he could name every kind of Rust-Oleum in the store. He listed the different colors of primer paint. He lovingly lined up the windshield wipers that had fallen on the ground. "Please let me come back," he said.

Finally, the guy gave in. Dad could come back to the store as soon as he'd finished paying off all the damage we'd done. Reese, Dewey, and I weren't allowed back until we were twenty-five.

And only if we didn't bring Hitchcock.

CHAPTER SIX

The next morning was Sunday and we had the whole day to work on Truck of Doom in the garage. As I got dressed, I glanced over at Hitchcock 2 in his cage. There was something stuck between the bars. I leaned over and pulled it out. It was a little bird finger puppet — one of Dewey's. He'd been talking to Hitchcock since we got back from the auto supply store. Now he was pestering Mom and Dad to get him a pet that talked. That would be great. A pet that could tell on me all the time just like Dewey.

"Malcolm," Hitchcock 2 said. I jumped. Who taught this bird my name? As if I had to ask.

"Look, I said I would take care of you. I didn't say I wanted to be friends," I said. "Don't talk to me."

I turned my back on the cage, but I felt him watching me. Then I could swear he made a vacuum cleaner sound. I spun around. "What do you know?" I demanded.

"Nevermore," said Hitchcock 2.

"Look, it was an accident," I said. "I didn't mean it."

"Take the cannolies," said Hitchcock 2.

I stared at him for a second. Then I realized I was

losing it. Hitchcock 2 was just a parrot. He didn't know what he was saying. There was no way he could know what happened to Hitchcock 1. I went outside to build my Truck of Doom.

As I stepped of the house, I felt something heavy and warm drop on my shoulder. A rogue cardinal flew off. "I just can't get a break," I said, looking at the bird poop on my shoulder. I hate birds.

I went to the bathroom and washed my shirt. It seemed like no matter how hard I scrubbed? I couldn't get the spot out. Finally I tossed the shirt in the hamper and went to my room to get a new one. When I got in there I found Reese sitting in the chair by his desk.

"Why aren't you out in the garage?" I asked.

"I had something to finish first," said Reese, holding up a sheet of paper. He was sucking a jawbreaker, so when he talked? It sounded like he had a mouthful of cotton or something. "I made you this list," Reese said. "Look it over."

I took the list and read it. There were about twenty-eight new chores on it for me to do, including all of Reese's homework. The last chore was: ANYTHING REESE WANTS.

"I think it's very reasonable," Reese said. "Under the circumstances. In exchange for my silence, you give me your cooperation. It's an offer you can't refuse."

Just what I didn't need. My very own godbrother.

In your dreams, I thought, putting the paper in my pocket. "Whatever," I said.

Happy at how well our meeting had gone, Reese strolled out and left me to find another shirt to wear. As I pulled it over my head, I heard a parrot voice behind me singing:

"Tell your mom or tell your dad

You made a mistake and you've been bad.

You'd better do what you've been taught

'Cause you're gonna get caught, you're gonna get caught."

What did I do to deserve this?

Oh yeah.

I ran out to the garage. When I got out there, Dad was reading from the mini-monster-truck driver's handbook. "No driver shall call time-out unless he's bleeding or unconscious. Then one of his partners may call time-out." Dad turned to Dewey. "That will be your job, son," he said. "Reese is usually the one who ends up unconscious."

Reese smiled modestly.

"Malcolm," said Dad, holding up the plans. "I think I found a way to make Truck of Doom even more intimidating. Look."

Dad pulled out a plastic skull. When he turned it on the eyes flashed red, the jaw opened and shut, and it laughed. There was something about that laugh I didn't like. If parrots could laugh, they would sound like that.

"That's excellent," said Reese.

"You bet it is," Dad agreed. "Look at Malcolm. He looks like he's seen a ghost."

I did not look like that.

We got through the day with only a few disasters. Like when Dad turned on the lawnmower motor Stevie had lent us? It started spinning around in a circle and Dad jumped away and knocked over Reese. Then Dewey sat on the decals and spent the rest of the day walking around with a sticker that said WIDE LOAD on his butt. Then I stepped on the rake and it flipped up and smacked me in the face. That part wasn't so funny.

By the time Mom called us in for dinner, we had ourselves a mini-monster truck. The HAUT BRION crates were now painted black with orange flames. We even attached spikes to the golf cart wheels. I couldn't wait to learn how to drive it.

"Did you guys finish your go-cart?" Mom asked as she set down a big plate of SpaghettiOs Primavera.

"It's not a go-cart, Lois," my dad corrected. "It's a lean, mean mini-truck machine that's going to strike fear in the hearts of all who see her and haunt their dreams for years to come."

"That's nice," said Mom. "You've got tomato sauce on your chin."

"I'm going to drive Truck of Doom, too," Dewey announced.

Dad was going to teach all of us during the week.

"If your feet can reach the pedals," I said.

"My feet reach the pedals," Dewey insisted.

"Last summer at Super Happy Funworld," Reese said, "we let you ride the bumper cars. You got stuck in the corner and wet your pants."

"I did not!" said Dewey.

"Of course not," I said. "Your shorts were always that color."

"Malcolm," Mom said warningly. Mom didn't like it when we made fun of Dewey wetting his pants. She said we would scar him for life.

Hey, maybe that's why he's still wearing those Daisy the Cow Puppet pajamas?

"The point is, he can't drive," I said.

"All of my boys can drive," Dad said. "It's part of your destiny."

In case you haven't noticed? My dad's really into race cars. He even named me after Rusty Malcolm, his favorite stock car racer.

"Mom," I said, "Francis is coming to the truck rally, isn't he?"

"That's up to Francis," Mom said. "If he doesn't get in trouble before then he can come."

I swallowed. Mom still didn't know that Francis was in trouble at school. He drove an armored tank into a lake. It was totally not his fault. That tank was supposed to be an all-terrain vehicle. How was he supposed to know it couldn't float? It was so unfair. But Francis would get himself out of trouble somehow. Just like I did.

As I climbed into bed Sunday night, everything

seemed to be falling into place. We had an excellent Truck of Doom. I had complete faith that Francis would find a way to salvage the tank or at least explain why he shouldn't have to. Sure, Reese thought I was his slave now, but tomorrow I would be getting rid of the parrot. No one would ever know that Hitchcock 1 had ceased to be. Lying in my bed, I closed my eyes and smiled.

"Malcolm," Hitchcock 2 said quietly from his cage. "Malcolm."

I didn't sleep much after that. But who needs sleep? Hitchcock 2 would be out of my hair the next day. I'd get some sleep after that. I guess I've been letting this get to me more than I realized.

Really, it was Mom's fault. If she hadn't brought home that super-sucker vacuum? I wouldn't have accidentally sucked the bird into it. No wait, it was Flor's fault. If she wasn't allergic to everything in the world? She would have had Hitchcock 1 this weekend. Or maybe it was Lloyd and Dabney's fault. They should really have been more careful with that Polophelus Heptamaculatus. And come to think of it, that Polophelus Heptamaculatus has a lot to answer for. It's certainly not my fault.

So why does that parrot keep saying my name?

CHAPTER SEVEN

"Malcolm, you're up early," my mom said when I walked into the kitchen. "What's the occasion?"

All I had to do was get past Mom and I'd be home free. I had to play this right.

"I couldn't sleep," I said. No, wait. Only guilty people can't sleep. "I mean I have a big test today." No, wait. Then why wasn't I studying all weekend? "I'm going jogging." No, wait. That's stupid.

"All right, what'd you break?" Mom said. She didn't even have to use her super truth-seeking powers to see that I was lying this time. I choked so bad it was embarrassing.

"Honest, Mom, I didn't break anything. I just need to get to school early."

"Yeah, right," said Mom, putting a frosted cinnamon Pop-Tart in the toaster for me. "I'll find out eventually."

As I ate my Pop-Tart, I wondered why I couldn't lie to my mom about killing a parrot. I had no trouble telling Dewey that he wasn't really my brother because my parents had just bought him from some trolls. (That explained his ears.) I thought about that as I made myself a second Pop-Tart. It was the last one in the box. I should get up early more often.

I was waiting outside the trailer with Hitchcock 2 when my teacher came to open it up. "Well, hi, Malcolm," she said.

Oh God, she knows! I thought. Then I realized that was stupid. She couldn't know. I had a parrot that looked just like the one I took home. Except for that one extra black dot on his chin. I'd noticed it as I left the house. But my teacher wouldn't notice it. Nobody would.

"Good morning, Hitchcock," my teacher said, uncovering the cage. She bent down and looked right at him and still couldn't tell the difference.

Suddenly I had a bad thought. What if the parrot decided to squeal on me right there? After a long pause he finally said, "Good morning, barf bag." I let out the breath I had just noticed that I was holding.

"Same old Hitchcock," the teacher chirped, letting us into the trailer. I stuck Hitchcock 2 in Hitchcock 1's regular spot and then ran back to my desk. I pretended to get really into my math homework. When the other kids started coming in, I watched to see if they noticed a difference in the parrot. They didn't. Stevie rolled over to me.

"So . . . how . . . did . . . it . . . go . . . this . . . weekend?" he asked.

"What do you mean?" I asked a little too quickly. "It was just a parrot, it was no big deal. Why would you ask me that?"

"Dude ... chill ... out," said Stevie. "I ... meant ... did ... you ... build ... Truck ... of ... Doom."

"Oh," I said. I tried to laugh but it sounded more like a squawk. "Truck of Doom is really cool. Yeah." My eyes drifted to the parrot cage again. Dabney, Lloyd, Eraserhead, and Martin were all crowded around it. Even Flor, who was still a little puffy but looked okay, was walking toward it. Had they all noticed something? I hurried over to the cage. When I got there I saw Hitchcock 2 leaned to the left on his perch. Hitchcock 1 always leaned to the right. How could I not have seen that before? Somebody would notice it for sure.

"If he looks different it's probably because my brothers have that effect on birds," I said casually. "It's nothing to worry about. So you can all get away from the cage now."

Nobody got away from the cage. Why weren't they getting away from the cage?

"Malcolm," my teacher said. "I know you've gotten attached to Hitchcock after having him at your house — everyone does. But we're just getting ready to work on his poetry skills."

Oh yeah. Remember how I said we were teaching him poetry? Monday morning was when we recited to him. It didn't matter if Hitchcock 2 didn't know any poetry. Hitchcock 1 never remembered anything we taught him.

First Lloyd got up and recited something from *Macbeth*. "It will have blood; they say, blood will have blood: Stones have been known to move, and trees to speak."

Okay, *Macbeth* is this play by William Shakespeare? About a guy who kills someone and then freaks out about it and ends up getting killed by trees. It's a long story.

Hitchcock 2 picked his beak with his talon. He looked bored.

Then Martin got up and recited from "The Raven." "Take thy beak from out my heart, and take thy form from off my door! Quoth the Raven, Nevermore."

Okay, "The Raven" is a poem by Edgar Allan Poe about a guy and this bird he can't ever get rid of. Hitchcock 2 seemed to like that poem, because he flapped his wings and bobbed his head to it like it was hip-hop.

"Interesting," said Martin. "Last week he preferred Shakespeare."

Uh-oh, I thought. *They're on to me*. I decided to deny everything. They couldn't pin anything on me. Let them try.

"How could his tastes have changed that much in one weekend?" asked Eraserhead, puzzled.

Stevie grinned at me. "What'd ... you ... do ... to ... him?"

Okay, *that* was an accusation.

"Nothing!" I yelled. "How should I know why he likes that poem? Why is everybody asking me? Are you accusing me of something? Am I the parrot's keeper?"

"Actually," said Martin, looking me up and down, "you were."

"This ... weekend," Stevie added. "Remember?"

I took a deep breath. It was possible I was letting my imagination run away with me. None of them knew this wasn't the bird I went home with Friday afternoon. But if I kept acting like a psycho, they'd figure it out. *Be cool, Malcolm,* I said to myself. *Be cool.*

I smiled at the class. "Just kidding," I said. That should do it.

Hitchcock 2 started reciting his own poem. "Tell your mom or tell your dad you made a mistake and you've been bad. You'd better do what you've been taught 'cause you're gonna get caught, you're gonna get caught."

Hitchcock had never recited anything on his own before, so the class was intrigued.

"Who wrote that, Gertrude Stein?" said Flor.

"It's Daisy the Cow Puppet," I muttered. I so hated that parrot.

The rest of the morning I tried to tell myself how

well I had handled this whole problem. That bird was a dead ringer. I mean, he was an alive ringer. Nobody could tell the difference. Except me. Every time I looked at Hitchcock 2 I relived the vacuum incident. *Shoomp!* I heard as I multiplied factors in algebra. *Gwaaaak!* I heard as I figured out the cosine of a triangle. When the lunch bell rang I heard, *Gwaaaak! Shoomp! Shoomp! Gwaaaak!*

That was weird. I ran out of the trailer. "Malcolm!" Hitchcock 2 said as I went past him.

I didn't stop running until I was in the middle of the playground. That's where I saw Reese waving me over.

"Malcolm," he said. "I need you to invite Tiffany Wigglesworth to have lunch with me. She's over by the water fountain."

I glanced across the playground and saw a tall girl with long hair giggling with some other girls. "Ask her yourself," I said.

I started to walk away but Reese stepped in front of me. "I must have heard you wrong, Muskrat," he said. "I thought Tiger asked you to do something. Did you forget about our deal?"

"Reese, it's over," I said. "The parrot's back in school. Nobody can tell the difference. I'm in the clear."

"Oh, you think so?" said Reese. "Because I don't think the teacher of your genius class would agree if I told her. If I told Mom, you could pretty much forget about having any fun for the rest of your childhood.

No matter where you go or what you do, I still know what you did last weekend."

While Reese was talking my brain was spinning, trying desperately to come up with something that would get me out of this. Basically it came down to having the rest of my childhood ruined by Mom or by Reese. I went with Reese.

"I'll be waiting over at that table," Reese said. "You will stand next to us while we eat in case we need anything. You will begin by picking all the green peppers out of Tiffany's Sloppy Joe."

This was going to be a long childhood.

When lunch was finally over and I was back in the trailer, Stevie rolled up next to me. "What's . . . up?" he asked. "Since . . . when . . . are . . . you . . . Reese's . . . butler?"

"I don't know what you're talking about," I said.

"I think what Stevie means is that you spent all of lunch running errands for your brother — a brother that you don't even like," said Dabney.

"It wasn't that bad," I mumbled.

"Malcolm, when he dropped a Frito you crawled under the table to get it for him!" yelled Lloyd.

"He . . . must . . . really . . . have . . . something . . . on . . . you," said Stevie.

"What?" I said. My palms were starting to sweat. "He does not. What could he possibly have on me?"

From the corner, Hitchcock 2 let out a bloodcurdling squawk. "It was an accident!" he screeched. "I didn't mean it! I didn't mean it!"

The other Krelboynes looked at each other, surprised by the bird's new vocabulary.

"Where'd he learn that?" I asked as if I had no idea. Hitchcock squawked again. "Dewey, get that pencil out of your ear!"

CHAPTER EIGHT

I wanted to run home right after school but I had to wait for Stevie. We always walked home together.

"I . . . just . . . need . . . to . . . finish . . . this . . . lab . . . report," he said when I came to his desk.

I went back to my desk to wait for him. I could see the parrot watching me. "You're gonna get caught," he sang. "You're gonna get caught."

"I'll meet you outside," I muttered to Stevie as I headed for the door.

The playground was pretty empty. I found a bench by the jungle gym and sat down on it. The shadow of the jungle gym bars crisscrossed the ground in front of me. I started thinking about the mini-truck rally. Dad had said he would come home early and teach us to drive Truck of Doom.

I looked down at the shadow of the jungle gym. The shadow of a bird landed on it. I turned around and looked at it. It was a crow. A big crow with shaggy black feathers like a vampire cape. It looked down at me over his sharp, black beak. What was it doing there? Maybe it was going to swoop down and jab its razor-beak into my head! Whoa, get a hold of yourself, Malcolm. It's just sitting there. Birds are always perching on things. I turned back around.

Not to brag, but I thought I'd be the best driver. Dad probably wouldn't even need to teach me, because it would come naturally. After all, I designed Truck of Doom, so I knew how it was supposed to work. I glanced down at the shadow again. Now there were two birds.

The thing with Reese is that he's too impatient. In bumper cars he's really good at hitting people? But he doesn't maneuver well. Dewey, on the other hand, is hopeless. He gets turned around backwards and has to spin twenty times before he's facing the right way again.

I heard a crow screech overhead and looked down at the jungle gym shadow.

It was totally filled with birds. Like, hundreds. They were jostling each other to make room and craning their necks to get a look at me, the bird murderer. I turned around fast. The jungle gym was empty.

That was a relief. I wasn't being stalked by birds; I was just crazy.

"Hey . . . Malcolm!" Stevie wheezed as he came out of the trailer. "Let's . . . roll."

As we went down the sidewalk, Stevie told me about the radiation experiment he was doing. I wasn't really listening. I was looking up in the trees. I'd never noticed how many birds there were.

There's this big oak tree? On the corner? I saw a blue jay in it, hiding behind some leaves. As soon as I saw it, it flew away. Then the same thing happened with a blackbird in an elm tree and a pigeon on a mailbox.

"Hey, Stevie," I said. "Do you know anything about birds?"

Stevie looked at me seriously. "Ornithology . . . happens . . . to . . . be . . . my . . . avocation."

Sometimes I really worry about Stevie. "Okay," I said. "So you can tell me. Do different kinds of birds talk to each other? Like could a parrot talk to a blue jay or a pigeon?"

Stevie laughed. "No," he said. If . . . they . . . could . . . we . . . wouldn't . . . have . . . a . . . chance."

"What do you mean, we wouldn't have a chance?" I asked. That didn't sound good.

"Well," said Stevie. "There . . . are . . . 8,650 . . . species . . . of . . . birds . . . in . . . the . . . world. Five . . . billion . . . 750 . . . million . . . birds . . . in . . . the . . . U.S. . . . alone. . . . More . . . than . . . 100 . . . billion . . . in . . . the . . . world. . . . If . . . they . . . got . . . to gether . . . we're . . . toast."

It didn't take long for me to do the math. Five billion, 750 million to two. The two were me and Reese. If the birds attacked, I was taking him down with me as a collaborator.

"Usually . . . they . . . go . . . for . . . the . . . eyes," Stevie continued. "Peck . . . peck . . . peck."

I walked faster. My house was in sight.

"Ever . . . heard . . . of . . . archaeopteryx?" Stevie asked. "The . . . link . . . between . . . birds . . . and . . . dinosaurs? He . . . rocked . . . the . . . Jurassic . . . Period." He waved at the unseen birds in the trees all around us. "Razor . . . sharp . . . teeth . . . long . . . bony . . . tail . . . three . . . claws . . . on . . . the . . . wing . . . to . . . crush . . . his . . . prey. . . . Feathers . . . wings . . . wishbone . . . These . . . are . . . his . . . people."

I felt a familiar warm, wet plop — this time on my head. "This is the second time one of archaeopteryx's people has pooped on me in two days," I said.

"Some . . . people . . . say . . . that's . . . good . . . luck," Stevie said.

"Yeah, I feel real lucky," I said, turning into my driveway. Reese was setting up an obstacle course for us to train on with Truck of Doom. I went inside to wash my head. Mom was in the kitchen arguing with someone on the phone.

"I don't know what you're talking about, Craig," she was saying.

Craig was a guy my mom worked with. He was nice but a little weird.

"Look, all I know was the vacuum was fine the last time I saw it," said Mom. I froze. "If it's having trouble sucking, something must be stuck in it. . . . How would I know what? The biggest thing it could have sucked up around here was Dewey and I just saw him. . . . Yes, I'm sure it was him. I know my own son, Craig!"

I started to back into my room, but my mom saw me.

"I have to go, Craig. Malcolm's here," she said. I could hear Craig still talking when Mom hung up the phone. Mom gave a big sigh. "Can you believe that?" she asked me. "They're having trouble with the super-sucker at work and they're trying to blame it on me because I had it last weekend. I mean, who knows what somebody might have sucked into it since then? Last month somebody vacuumed up a big hemorrhoid-cream spill in aisle six. You can bet it wasn't sucking real well after that."

I knew what was clogging that vacuum and it wasn't hemorrhoid cream. Somebody was going to get a big surprise when they opened that super-sucker up.

"You were the last one to use it, Malcolm," Mom went on, giving me a playful poke in the ribs. "You sure you didn't suck anybody into it?"

"What?!" I squeaked. "I was just vacuuming like you said!"

"Malcolm, calm down," Mom laughed. "I was just kidding. You've been jumpy ever since you brought that parrot home. I don't think you're cut out for pets."

I managed to smile as I backed into my room and shut the door. I looked over at my desk where the cage had been sitting. There was birdseed spilled on it. I swept it off onto the rug with my hand. I tried to grind it into the shag so I couldn't see it. I almost went to get the vacuum cleaner. That's when I heard the fluttering of wings outside my window. I looked out but I couldn't see any birds. They must have been hiding. It wasn't my imagination.

I did see my dad's car pull into the driveway. I ran into the bathroom and stuck my head under the faucet. By the time I got the bird poop out, Dad was ready to start teaching.

"You must be one with the car," Dad said when my brothers and I were assembled in the garage. "You must focus. You must not flinch. That is the way of the mini-monster-truck driver."

First Dad had Dewey get into the car and stuck a helmet on his head. It kept slipping down over his eyes? So Dad stuffed a baseball glove into it so it stayed up. Dad rolled him out to the beginning of the obstacle course. There were lines of orange rubber cones we had to drive through, ten cones in all. "Reese, where'd you get these?" Dad asked.

"They were just on the street," Reese said. "Next to that big hole."

"That's so people don't fall into it, son," Dad explained. "We'll bring them back when we're finished."

Reese shrugged. "Whatever."

Dad leaned down over Dewey, who was getting ready to drive. "Head down," he instructed. "Hands at ten o'clock and two o'clock." Dewey looked confused, so Dad placed his hands in the right places on the steering wheel. "Pedal check?"

"Right is go, left is stop," said Dewey.

"Very good, Dewey," said Dad. Then he took a red marker out of his pocket and drew an *R* on Dewey's right hand and an *L* on Dewey's left hand.

"Thanks!" said Dewey. And he was off.

Dewey didn't do as bad as I thought he would do. He knocked down all but one of the cones, but he stayed facing the right direction and he didn't wet his pants. Dad gave him a high five when he got out.

"My turn!" Reese yelled, grabbing the helmet off Dewey's head and lifting him off the ground in the process. "I feel the need for speed," Reese said as he took off. Reese left five cones standing and he would have left more if he learned to use the brake. It's like I said, he likes hitting things.

"Malcolm?" my dad said when Reese finished doing his victory dance. "The helmet is yours."

I climbed into Truck of Doom. I could smell the fresh paint. We'd made a flag showing a four-headed tiger and it was flapping in the breeze. The wheel was warm in my hands. I stepped on the accelerator. It sounded like a vacuum. My skin started to prickle.

As I approached the first cone, it turned into a big orange parrot and came flapping at me. I jerked the wheel to get away from it and knocked over a cone with the front of the car. The back of the car knocked over another cone and I spun out into three more. I just wanted to get away from the parrots, so I drove straight through the next three cones. They flew up in the air and then fell down as if they were dive-bombing me. I took my hands off the wheel to protect myself and knocked down the last two cones. Then I hit the gas and roared over the front lawn.

The next thing I knew I was in the kitchen with the motor still running. My mom was staring at me with her mouth open. A bag of hot-dog buns dangled from her hand. Moments later my dad, Reese, and Dewey came running in. I turned off the ignition.

"Malcolm," Dad said, bending over and putting his hand on my shoulder. "That was the worst driving I've ever seen in my life."

CHAPTER NINE

For the next two days my life was just one big series of "driving your car into the kitchen" jokes. You wouldn't think there'd be that many? But my family found them all.

"Hey Malcolm, are you going to sit at the table for breakfast or do you want to use the drive-thru?" Mom asked on Tuesday morning.

"Where'd you find a parking space?" Reese asked when I came into dinner on Tuesday night.

At dinner on Wednesday, Dewey announced, "There was this boy in my class. He drove a car to school. He parked it on the roof."

"He did not," I muttered.

The worst was my dad. He didn't make any jokes. He just shook his head sadly whenever he saw me.

After dinner I just went to my room. I had to get started on Reese's homework. It was a lot harder to do than my own homework because I had to pretend it wasn't easy. If Reese got an A? My cover would be blown. As I was finishing Reese's essay on "What I want to be when I grow up" (according to my essay Reese wanted to be a cocktail waitress), the phone rang. I was ready for a break, so I answered it.

"Young Master Malcolm!"

"Francis!" I said. "What's up?" Boy, was I glad to hear from him. Francis wouldn't make fun of me for driving into the kitchen. After all, he just drove a tank into a lake. And Francis would know just what to do to get the birds to stop following me and to get Reese off my back. All I needed to do was talk to Francis for five minutes and all my problems would be solved.

"Boy, do I have problems," Francis announced.

Wait. What?

"The school will not get off my back about this tank," Francis said. "It was an accident, for God's sakes. I didn't mean it."

I knew just how Francis felt. "You didn't do it on purpose," I said.

"Of course not," said Francis. "I didn't even want to go near that tank. They made me wash it for breaking curfew seven nights in a row."

I didn't want to go near that parrot, either. "None of this would have happened if they'd just left you alone," I said.

"That's all I ask," said Francis. "Really, it's like *they* drove the tank into the lake. Not me."

"Right," I said. "It's all their fault. So why do I still feel . . . I mean, why do *you* still feel guilty?"

There was a beat of silence on the other end.

"I don't feel guilty," said Francis. "I feel maligned, falsely accused, and victimized by a corrupt system of justice, but I don't feel guilty."

"Really?" I said. So why did I feel guilty? Maybe Francis couldn't help me after all. "But if you did feel guilty, what would you . . . ?"

I felt a tap on my shoulder. It was Reese.

"Malcolm," he said. "Is that Francis you're talking to?"

"Yeah," I said impatiently.

"Great," said Reese. "Hand over the phone."

"No way," I said. "Wait till I'm . . ."

Before I could finish Reese started making parrot noises and flapping his arms in my face. I threw the phone at him and stomped back down the hall to our room. Maybe I should make Reese a proctologist. That way when the teacher asked him to read his essay? He wouldn't even be able to pronounce his chosen profession.

When I opened the door, I found Dewey sitting in front of a soggy paper plate. In the middle of the plate was a rotten apple and the apple was swarming with bugs. There were ants, some rainbow-colored beetles, a few sickly white mealworms, a few bottle-green horseflies, and one giant millipede sliding around on a thousand feet. I'm sure there were a lot of other things I just couldn't see. Luckily, I was pretty sure there weren't any *Polophelus Heptamaculata* there, unless Dewey had been to the Amazon recently.

Dewey was kneeling in front of the plate, wearing finger puppets of a horse and a cow. At first I thought he was putting on a show. Then I realized he was trying to teach the bugs to talk like Hitchcock.

"Say hi, Dewey," he was saying. "Hi, Dewey. Hi, Dewey. Now you try it."

The bugs just kept crawling over the apple. Two of the beetles locked pincers in battle and tumbled onto the plate. I considered telling Dewey that bugs don't have vocal cords and the only way they'd ever say "Hi, Dewey" would be if they got into formation and spelled it out on the wall. But it was more fun watching Dewey try to teach them. I thought the mealworm looked genuinely confused.

"Don't worry, guys," Dewey said, putting his face next to the apple. "Hitchcock is a parrot and he learned how to talk. He'll be coming back soon to teach everyone to talk. Very soon. He's my friend and he promised. When he comes back, we'll go to the zoo. We'll teach all the animals to talk. I'll tell the elephant to sit on Reese. Then he'll be sorry."

I felt a chill go up my spine. Not because of the elephant. Because of what Dewey said about Hitchcock coming back. I knew Hitchcock wasn't *really* coming back. Now if I could just convince my spine of that. I left Dewey to his bugs and went into the kitchen. Mom was washing dishes at the sink, listening to the radio and singing: "'I didn't know if it was day or night, I started kissing everything in sight, until I kissed a cop down on Thirty-fourth and Vine ...'"

"Mom?" I said.

She turned and kept singing. "'He broke my little bottle of Love Potion Number Nine.' What's up, Malcolm?"

"I was wondering ..."

Mom threw a towel at me. It landed on my head.

"If you're gonna talk, make yourself useful," she said. "I'll wash and you dry."

I stood next to Mom at the sink, and she turned down the radio that was on that station that only played songs from before I was alive. "I was wondering," I began. "I mean, I have this friend ... I mean, I'm doing a thing for school? So I'm supposed to ask this." I was off to a great start.

"Spit it out," Mom encouraged.

"Have you ever done something — something bad — that you didn't mean to do? I mean, it was an accident?"

"Did your brother Francis have another accident?" said Mom. "Because I know all about his 'accidents.' If he's done something wrong he's going to have to suffer for it. Since he doesn't have the sense to feel bad about the things he does, society has to make him feel bad."

I had no idea what Mom was talking about. "So anyway, about my problem," I said. "I mean my friend's problem. If it was an accident and you didn't get caught? Would you tell anyone? Remember, there's no way you're going to get caught and it wasn't even your fault."

Mom turned off the faucet and looked at me. "What'd you do?" she asked.

"Nothing!" I said. "I told you, it was my friend."

"You told me it was a thing for school," she corrected me.

"That's right. It's a thing for a friend at school. You don't know him. He's not even really my friend. He's not even really at school. He's our class pen pal from Mozambique. Anyway, do you think he should confess?"

"If he doesn't I'll find out anyway," Mom said.

I felt my eyes get wide. "How are you going to find out what happened in Mozambique?" I asked.

"Malcolm, I find out everything, eventually," Mom said. "No matter where you go, no matter what you do, you can't hide it from me. Don't you remember that time you were five and you spilled paint all over your teacher's fake fur coat?"

My mouth went dry. "You know about the Dead Muppet Coat?" I croaked.

"I know everything," said Mom. "Now finish the dishes."

Mom left me to scrape the last of the Ravioli Helper off the pots. That's the great thing about fast food. You just throw out the plates and the plastic forks. I don't know why people ever make their own food. I tossed the dish towel back onto the counter and went back to my room. Hopefully Dr. Dewey-little was finished talking to the animals — I mean, insects — by now.

My dad was already in there with Dewey. "No," Dewey was saying. "They're my friends! You don't throw friends out the window!"

"Dewey, the bugs like being outside," Dad explained. "I'll take them right back to their families so they'll be safe and sound."

Dewey sighed and kneeled down to his bugs. "Sorry you can't sleep over," he said. "I'll come see you tomorrow. Don't forget to practice: Hi, Dewey."

"I'm sure they will, son," Dad said. "You're a good friend."

Dewey went into the bathroom to brush his teeth. As soon as Dewey shut the door, Dad scooped up the plate, ran to the window, and chucked it as far as he could into the neighbor's yard. Then he wiped his hands like he could still feel the bugs crawling on them.

"He's just going through a phase," Dad said. He shuddered as he walked out.

Dewey's phases were always wet, sticky, or smelly. Sometimes all three.

When Dewey came back into our bedroom and saw the bugs were gone, he shrugged. "It's okay," he said. "Hitchcock's coming back. He'll teach them all to talk."

I was about to tell him Hitchcock wasn't coming back. Then I heard a scraping sound at the window like a talon scratching on the glass.

You know, the more I think about it? The more I think animals shouldn't talk. What do they really have to say?

Some people shouldn't talk, either. Like Reese. When it was time to go to sleep? He made me turn down the covers on his bed and fluff his pillow. Then he wanted a glass of water that he took one sip of. Then he made me read to him from <u>TV Guide</u> so he would know all the shows he was missing while he was at school. Then he waited until I was in bed to make me get him another blanket. He didn't even use it. He said it was just in case.

I picked up my pillow to slug him and he made vacuum sucking noises. I was going to smack him anyway but I heard a bird outside the window. I think it was a pigeon. Maybe it was a vulture. Maybe it was Hitchcock, come back to teach everyone to talk.

CHAPTER TEN

That night I dreamed I went to the linen closet and the super-sucker was inside. It turned on by itself and started chasing me down the hall. I tried to warn everyone to get out of its way but it was too late. *Shoomp!* Dewey got sucked into the nozzle. *Shlump!* There went Reese — that part of the dream was okay. But then Mom and Dad went down — *SHOOMP! SHOOMP!* The doorbell rang. It was Francis! Riding a tank! "Francis, stay back!" *Shoomp!* Too late. All that was left was the tank, Francis's cadet's hat, and a bag of dirty laundry.

I turned and faced the vacuum that was coming right for me. Now I saw who was controlling it. It was Hitchcock, only he was part dinosaur now, like archaeopteryx. And he was screeching, "You're gonna get caught! You're gonna get caught!" through his razor-sharp teeth.

Then I was on the set of *Mr. Wiffle's Playhouse?* Being interviewed by Daisy the Cow Puppet about fruit bats. I don't know why. Dreams are weird like that.

The birds woke me up the next morning. They were outside my window. They were pretending to be singing but I knew they were coming to get me.

"Malcolm, why are you pouring syrup into your orange juice?" my mom asked at breakfast. Yeah, that's what I was doing.

"I don't know," I said, putting the syrup down.

Reese came in, hit me on the head and sat down. I started waving my arms and yelling, "No! No! Get off!"

"What's the matter with Malcolm?" Dewey asked.

"I'm fine," I said. "I thought a bird landed on my head, that's all."

Dad looked around the kitchen to make sure there were no birds. "All clear, son," he said.

"Dude, there's no birds in the kitchen," said Reese, shoveling scrambled eggs into his mouth.

"Shhh!" I hissed. Everyone got quiet. I could hear two robins outside the window. I thought they were talking about me. "Hear them?" I said. "They're everywhere."

"Who is?" asked Mom.

"The birds," I said.

There was a silence. I saw Mom and Dad giving each other that *Should we be worried about this?* look. Finally Dewey said, "Are the birds going to eat us?"

"No," Reese smirked. "Just Malcolm."

"Shut up!" I yelled, running out of the kitchen with my hands over my ears. Dad drove Dewey to school that morning. My parents wanted Reese to walk with me because they thought I was acting peculiar for some reason.

"You can drop the act now," said Reese when we left the house. "You're still my slave."

I wasn't really listening to Reese? Because I'd spotted a couple of blackbirds on a tree branch. "What are you looking at?" I yelled at them. "You wanna piece of me?"

The blackbirds opened their beaks and made noises that sounded like truck horns? They were probably some kind of bird swear words. Then they flew away over the rooftops.

"Quit the psycho routine," Reese said. "I'm not buying it. You still have to — hey, where are you going?"

I ran ahead down the street. There were these two little brown birds drinking out of a puddle. They looked innocent. I'm sure that's why they were sent to spy on me. "Look, it was an accident," I told them. "I didn't mean it." The brown birds didn't listen. Reese came up beside me.

"You're taking all the fun out of this for me," he said. "You ruin everything."

"Get down!" I yelled, pulling Reese to the sidewalk and throwing myself on top of him. A crow dipped down — dangerously close. "Okay, he's gone," I said, getting back up.

Reese brushed himself off and eyed me suspiciously. "Dude," he said. "Get some help."

Some thanks I get for saving his life from that crow assassin.

Hitchcock 2 was waiting for me when I came into the trailer. He said, "Polly want a cracker?"

"That's it!" I said, walking up to the cage. "Look, stop talking to me and tell your friends to back off!"

Everybody turned around and looked at us. I'll bet Hitchcock felt stupid now.

"Malcolm, maybe you should sit down," my teacher said nervously.

"Yes, come sit down, Malcolm," Martin said, pulling out one chair and then another one. "Put your feet up."

I sat down, putting my feet on the other chair. Martin took out a pad. Stevie, Dabney, and Lloyd sat next to Martin. I could see the blank pad reflected in Stevie's glasses.

"How are we feeling today?" asked Martin.

We? "I'm fine," I said. "Never better."

In the reflection in Stevie's glasses I saw Martin write down CLASSIC DENIAL.

"No really, I'm fine," I said. "Everything's excellent. My brother Francis may be coming home this weekend and we're going to a truck rally. Francis is great. I wish my mom didn't send him to military school."

Martin wrote down MOTHER ISSUES?

"No, really. It wasn't Francis's fault. It was an accident."

Martin wrote down FRANCIS — HERO WORSHIP COMPLEX?

Now I was getting mad. "Look," I said. "There's nothing wrong with me. Now would somebody make those birds shut up?"

The other kids looked at one another. "What . . . birds?" asked Stevie.

"The ones outside," I said. "Hitchcock's friends. He's got them following me all over the place. They're always talking about me. Whispering. Chirping. I can't sleep!"

Martin wrote down LOONEY TUNES.

Now I was more angry than I was when Reese said he was going to take credit for designing Truck of Doom.

"What's wrong with all of you?" I yelled. "Can't you hear the birds right outside the window?"

For a second nobody said anything. Then Flor smiled gently and said, "I hear the birds, Malcolm." I sighed with relief. Flor continued, "I think they're telling you to see the school psychiatrist."

I ran screaming out of the trailer and all the way home.

Mom was on the phone with the school when I ran through the door. She turned around and stopped me in my tracks. She had her eyes set on STUN. "Thank you," she said into the phone. "He just walked in. I'll take it from here."

Mom hung up the phone. "So, Malcolm," she said, focusing her truth-gun eyes right at my heart. "Spill it."

I spilled like Niagara Falls. "I killed the parrot," I said.

Mom's eyes got wide.

"But I didn't mean it!" I said. "I was vacuuming, just like you said. And everything was clean. And then the bird threw seed all over and I turned on the vacuum to five by mistake and he was just gone."

"Gone?" Mom repeated.

"It was just — *shoomp!* Into the super-sucker he went."

"So that's what was clogging it," Mom said. "Then mister, you're going to replace that parrot and . . ." Mom stopped short and started to laugh. "You did replace it, didn't you, you little sneak!"

"Yeah," I admitted. "I sold my *Youngblood #27* and bought a parrot just like Hitchcock. I thought everything was taken care of? But it keeps getting worse and worse. I have to be Reese's slave to keep him quiet, and all the birds know what I did. They're everywhere. I haven't slept all week. I sold my *Youngblood #27* for nothing! What went wrong? Francis would never have this problem."

Mom put her hand on my shoulder. "That's why Francis has to go to military school and you can walk around free on the streets," she explained. "You've got a conscience. You know you did something bad and you have to confess it."

"Tell your mom or tell your dad you've made a mistake and you've been bad," I said.

"You took the first step, Malcolm. You told your mom. Now you have to tell your genius class."

"Why do I have to tell them?" I asked. I thought telling Mom would fix everything. That's what Daisy the Cow Puppet clearly implied in her song.

"Because it's the Krelboyne parrot you rubbed out!" Mom said. "Those poor kids have been harboring a counterfeit parrot all week!"

"I guess so," I admitted.

"So here's what you have to do," Mom said. "Tomorrow you'll confess to your teacher, confess to your class — and apologize to that parrot for making him live a lie! I'll go to the Lucky Aid and perform a parrot-ectomy on the super-sucker."

"I don't know if I can tell everyone," I said.

"Your choice," Mom said. "But if you don't . . . you'll never sleep again."

CHAPTER ELEVEN

The next morning I stood in front of the mirror in the bathroom and practiced my confession to the Krelboynes. "Hi, my name is Malcolm and I'm a parrot murderer." No, they know my name. "Hey you guys, remember that parrot we used to have?" No, too casual. "I did it! I did it and I'd do it again!"

I splashed some cold water on my face. I was just going to have to wing it.

When I got outside Reese was waiting for me. He was smiling at me. "Reese, leave me alone," I said.

Reese took a step toward me.

"Reese, I mean it!" I yelled. "Cut it out. I'm really stressed out this morning!"

"Perfect!" said Reese. "Dude, that is so cool. Could you come over to my table at lunch? My whole class wants to meet Mad Malcolm."

"Who?" I said.

"That's you," said Reese. "Everybody knows about what you did yesterday. I heard how you flipped out in class. I heard the Krelboynes were so scared they had to be sedated. Did you really swing from the florescent lights hanging by your teeth?"

I stared at Reese. "What are you talking about?" I said.

Just then I noticed some kids walking by us. They pointed at me and whispered together. Then they hurried on ahead like they were afraid to get too close to me. Reese was looking at me with total admiration. Usually he had to beat up a kid to get that reaction.

"I didn't really do anything," I explained. "I just got a little freaked in class and ran out."

"Oh yeah," Reese said. "Like eating the frogs for science class is getting a little freaked. I heard you swallowed some of them live."

I looked around. All the kids on their way to school were watching me? But trying to look like they weren't watching me. For the first time in my life I was notorious. It was kind of cool.

"Do you want me to carry your books?" Reese asked. "Or are you thinking about tearing them apart with your teeth like you did with the encyclopedias in class?" He sounded hopeful.

"You can carry them," I said.

Hey, I'd carried his books all week. I was just getting payback here.

When I stepped into the trailer, all the furniture was moved around. "Malcolm," my teacher said nervously. "I'm rearranging the desks according to feng-shui principles. I think we've created a more soothing environment. Your desk is over there."

It was in the corner under a kitten poster that said "Hang in there!" There was a punching bag on a spring that I could hit when I was feeling "overwhelmed." For a second I thought I really was going crazy because I could hear whales singing. "It's a tape," Flor said. "Listening to humpback whales is supposed to lower your blood pressure."

I sat down at my new stress-free desk. The whole class was looking at me with these fake smiles they'd obviously been taught by the school psychiatrist. "How . . . are . . . we . . . today . . . Malcolm?" asked Stevie, keeping his wheelchair as far away from me as possible.

I might as well get this over with? Because I couldn't stand much more of being treated like a ticking time bomb. "Actually," I said, standing up and causing the rest of the class to take a step back, "I've got something to say."

I walked to the front of the class. My teacher smiled encouragingly. "We're here for you," she said. "I know you want to talk about what happened yesterday. Your little episode."

"You . . . went . . . postal," said Stevie.

"Hardly a scientific diagnosis," said Martin. "But accurate."

I took a deep breath. "I don't want to talk about yesterday," I said. "I want to talk about Saturday. That's when I killed the Krelboyne Parrot and none of you ever knew."

Hitchcock made a series of high-pitched squeals that sounded like violins? The kind you would hear when someone was getting killed in a scary movie.

The pencil my teacher was holding fell out of her hand and bounced on the floor.

"I'm sorry, Malcolm?" she said, her voice quivering in that way it did when she was trying to sound like she had everything under control? But she didn't? "What did you say?"

"He said he killed the parrot!" said Hitchcock 2. "Killed the parrot! Killed the parrot! Risselty-rosselty!"

"Yes, I killed the parrot!" I yelled.

You know how they talk about getting something off your chest? It really did feel like a big weight was off my chest. "It was an accident! I was vacuuming my room with a super-sucker my mom brought home from work. I accidentally put it on five."

"Good God!" Dabney gasped. "Do you have any idea how much sucking power that is?"

"I do now," I said. "I didn't even know I was pointing it in the bird's direction. The next thing I knew he was gone."

"So you're saying the parrot you went home with . . . expired?" my teacher asked.

How much more clear could I make it? "Yes," I said. "He's gone to meet his maker. He's a stiff. Pushing up the daisies. He's bought the farm."

"Shuffled off his mortal coil!" cried Hitchcock 2.

"*Hamlet*," said Lloyd proudly. "He's learning his Shakespeare."

My teacher still wasn't getting it. "So you're saying . . . "

"His . . . metabolic . . . processes . . . are . . . now . . . history," said Stevie. Finally, she seemed to understand.

"So then, who's that?" she asked, pointing to the other bird who was now picking his beak with his talon.

"I bought him at the pet store to replace the one I sucked into the vacuum," I said. "He looked just the same. I didn't think anyone would notice. I've been calling him Hitchcock 2."

"Actually," said Martin. "That would be Hitchcock 3. You vacuumed Hitchcock 2. I'm afraid the original Hitchcock met with an unfortunate accident at my house."

All eyes swiveled to look at Martin sitting at his desk. "I saw him eyeing my pet snake, Rupert, with interest and I warned him to stay away, but he didn't listen. When I returned to my room, he was gone and Rupert had a suspicious-looking bulge in his middle."

"So what did you do?" I asked him. I couldn't believe this! How come he wasn't freaking out in school and getting harassed by birds?

"Same thing you did, Malcolm," he said. "I replaced the bird with one I got at the pet shop. My mother paid for it. She didn't want Rupert implicated in any more scandals."

"Okay, then," I said. "It's Hitchcock 3."

I heard a sniffle to my left. Lloyd was crying. That was never good. "It's Hitchcock 4!" he gulped, between sobs. "There was a cotton-candy machine . . . sticky . . . feathers everywhere . . . oh, the horror!" Lloyd broke down completely.

"He called me completely hysterical," Dabney said, picking up the narrative for Lloyd. "I told him to have his mother take him to the mall and get a new parrot. That's what I did when I was taking care of Hitchcock and my zero-gravity experiments went terribly wrong."

"Wait a minute," I said. "You mean this is Hitchcock 5?"

"Hitchcock . . . 6."

I looked at Stevie and shook my head. "Et tu, Kenarban?" I said. That means "You too, Stevie?" in Latin.

Stevie hung his head. "My . . . mom . . . says . . . birds . . . carry . . . germs," he said. "She . . . kept . . . spraying . . . disinfectant . . . I . . . threw . . . up . . . he . . . died."

"So let me get this straight," I said, facing the class. "Every one of you killed this bird?"

"I didn't," said Flor. Then, so we wouldn't feel bad, she added, "But I'm sure I would have this weekend."

"Everybody who did kill the parrot, raise your hand," I said. When I finished counting, it turned out the bird in the corner was Hitchcock 19. That was one bird for almost everyone in the class, except one kid who killed him twice in one weekend!

My teacher seemed to get a shade paler every time someone else confessed. "Poor little things," she cried. "Beautiful plumage."

"Bite me!" Hitchcock 19 said from his cage. Then he threw a seed at Eraserhead.

"Cut it out!" Eraserhead yelled. "He did that to me all weekend at my house. That's why I put him outside. How did I know he'd freeze to death?"

"How about bird poop?" I said. "Did he throw bird poop at you?"

"It never stopped," Lloyd said, beating his head softly against his desk. "It never stopped."

"He called my grandmother a wrinkled-up monkey butt," said Martin. "Rupert has never been anything but polite to Grandmother."

"He made doorbell noises all night at my house," said Dabney. "My mother had to go away to a spa to recover."

Stevie was clenching his fists. "He . . . moved . . . all . . . my . . . intergalactic . . . soldiers . . . to . . . the . . . top . . . of . . . the . . . bookcase."

That didn't sound so bad. Then I realized Stevie didn't have a chance of reaching the top of his bookcase from his wheelchair. That was one nasty parrot. I mean, that was nineteen nasty parrots.

We spent the rest of the morning trading Hitchcock horror stories. Hitchcock 19 seemed to really love it, because he kept adding sound effects: blenders, garbage trucks, ladies screaming, jazz music, footsteps running down stairs — anything that fit the story. The only person who didn't have a story was Flor, but the teacher decided not to let her take the parrot home after all. From now on, Hitchcock 19 would spend the weekends with our teacher.

"We're going to have so much fun," the teacher said as she covered up his cage to take him home.

"That's what you think!" said Hitchcock 19.

"Isn't he cute?" she giggled.

Before I left I went over to Hitchcock 19's cage. I lifted the cover and stared at Hitchcock. "Look," I said. "I just want you to know I didn't mean it. And I'm sorry I made you live a lie."

Hitchcock 19 cocked his head. "Keep away," he squawked. "The sow is mine. Nicklety, knacklaty!"

"Whatever," I said. I was finally free.

Mom was right. I felt much better now that I'd confessed. I couldn't wait to tell her how all the other kids were murderers too.

When I got home, Mom was on the phone. "I've never seen him have a breakdown before, Doctor," she was saying. "At least not this bad. Even during the big Tic Tac spill."

I stopped to listen. If somebody was having a breakdown, Mad Malcolm wanted to know about it.

"I warned Craig what was inside the vacuum,"

Mom continued. "He's a grown man. I thought he could take it." There was a pause while the doctor talked. "Well, I wouldn't call it bloodcurdling carnage, but it was pretty gruesome," she said. "All those feathers."

When Mom got off the phone, she told me Craig had insisted on helping her "fix" the super-sucker. He took one look and started howling. Mom finally had to call the paramedics.

"I guess it was pretty gross," I said.

Mom nodded. "And you know the weirdest thing about it?" she said. "When I opened the vacuum bag I could swear that bird was flipping me off."

CHAPTER TWELVE

After dinner that night we made chili-pepper popcorn. I told everyone how the Krelboynes killed Hitchcock nineteen times.

"Hitchcock isn't coming back, is he?" Dewey sighed.

"Not if I can help it," I said. Then I explained how the birds had been keeping me under twenty-four-hour surveillance. And how that drove me insane.

Everyone thought the story was cool, especially my dad. "I knew there was a reason you couldn't drive," he said, pulling me into a big hug. "Racing is in your blood, boy."

It was kind of embarrassing getting hugged? So when the phone rang, I ran to get it.

"Francis!" I said when I answered it. "Are you at the bus station? Should we pick you up?"

"I'm at school," Francis said. He didn't sound happy.

"What?" I said. "What do you mean? You're supposed to be here for the mini-monster-truck rally tomorrow."

"You think I don't know that?" said Francis. "I was

halfway out the door when they took away my weekend pass . . . on Mom's orders!"

"Mom's orders?" I said. "But Mom didn't even know about the —"

I turned and looked at Mom over my shoulder. She was standing with her arms crossed over her chest.

"I find out everything, eventually," she reminded me. Mom took the phone out of my hand. No matter what I went through this week? It wasn't as bad as what Francis was going to get now. Dad, Reese, and Dewey all flinched as Mom took a deep breath and started yelling at Francis.

"Let's get out of here," Dad said. He pulled me out to the garage right then for another trial run, and Reese and Dewey came to watch. We didn't have the orange cones anymore, so my brothers stood in for them. "Okay," Dad said, putting the helmet on me. "Be one with the car."

This time I was awesome on the course. Even Reese was yelling, "Mad Malcolm, go!"

When it was over, Dad looked thoughtfully at Truck of Doom. "You know," he said. "I've got an idea."

We got to work right away repainting the car and making a new flag. This one had four parrots on it that all looked like Hitchcock. They were breathing fire and picking up other trucks in their talons. We added a killer beak to our laughing skull with the glowing red eyes. When we were finished, we had an official renaming ceremony.

"I dub thee The Parrotrooper," said Reese. "The ultimate bird of prey."

That night I slept. Usually I wouldn't mention that? But it had been a while, so it was kind of exciting for me. I said hi to the pigeons in the parking lot at the truck rally and they ignored me, just like pigeons should.

"How are you feeling?" my dad said when we got inside. We were doing our pre-race huddle where we chanted, "Parrotrooper, Parrotrooper, Parrotrooper, Parrotrooper!" There was a flash that broke our concentration.

"Mom!" I said. "No pictures while we're chanting!"

She put away her camera. "Come on," she said. "You all look so cute!"

We looked at our uniforms she'd made for us really fast last night. They were blue with feathers on the shoulders and torn to look like they were clawed by parrots. They were definitely not cute. But my mom's weird that way, so we posed for a picture with our mini-truck.

"Everyone to the starting gate!" the voice over the loudspeaker said. We ran to our places around the track. Each one of us was doing a leg of the race: first Dewey, then Reese, and then me. Dad was our pit coach. He pulled our helmets from his bag — he'd even managed to find one small enough for Dewey. It looked like a salad bowl with a strap? But Dad insisted it was a junior helmet. He lifted Dewey up and placed him in The Parrotrooper. From behind, I could see Dewey's driving name emblazoned on his uniform: DR. DEWEY-LITTLE. We figured since Dewey thought he could talk to animals and bugs? He could communicate with the mini-truck too. Dad's uniform said HOT WHEELS HAL.

The voice on the loudspeaker announced, "Gentlemen, start your engines!"

Dad pulled the cable on the Parrotrooper engine and it started up with a roar. I'll bet Stevie's lawnmower never sounded so cool. "Ready . . ."

Dewey gripped the wheel at the ten o'clock and two o'clock positions.

"Set . . ."

He checked his hands for which one was right and left.

"Go!"

Dewey peeled out. I have to admit? He was amazing. He didn't flinch once. If there were two cars ahead of him? He shot right through the middle.

"He's a master," my dad whispered.

"I don't buy it," said Reese.

Dewey rounded the track and came right at us. That was when we realized the salad bowl had slipped down over his eyes. He couldn't see where he was going.

"Brake! Brake!" my dad yelled to him. "Left pedal, Dewey! Left foot!"

Luckily, Dewey could still see the R and the L on his

shoes. He hit the brake and skidded to a stop. Dad pulled him out and Reese jumped in. He squealed back onto the track. I had barely enough time to read the back of his uniform: ROAD RAGE REESE.

We didn't even have to make up that nickname for Reese. It just fit him. Coming around the first time, some kid in a truck called Mark of Zorro came a little too close and Reese got personal. He chased the kid all over the track, knocking over the bales of hay that lined the perimeter.

"Get him!" yelled Mom from the sidelines. "Use your speed!"

"Be one with the car," Dad muttered, like he was trying to talk to Reese telepathically. The weird thing is? I think it worked. Reese pulled ahead and right into our pit stop. Now it was MAD MALCOLM'S turn. I checked my chin strap, tightened my seat belt, and burned rubber. I kept myself steady and my speed at full throttle. Dirt smacked the windshield as I neared the car in front of me. Just as I was about to make my move? Some guy in a green and black truck called The Viper totally cut me off.

I flinched and The Parrotrooper swerved a little. Now The Viper was in front of me and to pass I'd have to slip in between The Viper and the other truck, The Mighty Mongoose. I didn't know if I had the guts. Who would?

Hitchcocks 1 through 19, that's who.

I gripped my hands like talons on the wheel and screamed like a siren. "Bite me!!!!"

The Krelboyne Parrot

The two drivers ahead of me turned around for a second, scared. That's when I shot between them and took the lead. I came around past Mom, who was going crazy. "Mad Malcolm, go! Mad Malcolm, go!"

I never felt so good in my life? But now I had to focus. The finish line was up ahead. Dewey, Dad, and Reese were in a huddle, chanting "Parrotrooper! Parrotrooper!" when I flew in over the finish line and won it for us.

My team jumped all around me, and Dad tried to pull me out of the truck, but my hands were gripping the wheel so tightly? It took all three of them to pry them off. Then I was up on Dad's shoulders. He was right. Racing was in our blood.

After we got our silver hubcap, we all went to the snack bar outside for hot dogs. "See Malcolm?" Mom said. "You never would have won today if you hadn't come clean about that parrot."

"He probably would have ended up back in the kitchen," said Dad.

"Dad, can slugs talk?" asked Dewey.

"No, they can't, son," said Dad.

Mom frowned and leaned over to Dewey. Sure enough, there was a slug on his plate and he was offering it a french fry. Mom flicked it off with her fork.

"Back to the wild," she said. Dewey shrugged and ate the french fry himself. "Did you really think the birds were talking to you?" she asked me.

"Not really," I said.

Reese snorted. "Yes, really," he said. "You were a

legend. Even more than that kid who used to cover himself with paste in kindergarten so he could stick to the walls."

Great. Just the kind of legend I always wanted to be.

"Your brother isn't crazy," Mom said. "He was just hounded by guilt. That's a good thing. You kill a parrot, you should feel guilty, no matter how nasty it was."

I guess she was right.

"So everything's okay now," Mom wrapped up. "You've got a clean slate. Your conscience is clear and the birds aren't out to get you anymore."

I bit into my hot dog, but only got bread. I opened my bun, but there was nothing inside. "Who took my hot dog?" I said. Everyone was looking up. I followed their eyes into a tree, where a blue jay sat, finishing my hot dog.

Without a word, we all got up and moved to another table. We weren't taking any chances.

On Monday morning I felt pretty good. The Hitchcock thing was out in the open and I was wearing a T-shirt we got from the mini-monster-truck rally. I could hear Dewey watching Mr. Wiffle's Playhouse in the next room. Daisy the Cow Puppet was singing.

"Daisy the Cow Puppet is your friend
She wants to save you from a bad end,
So always listen to what Daisy has to say
Or you'll live to regret it one fine day."

Me and Reese went into the living room. I grabbed the remote and changed the channel. The Skeletrons had trapped the Ninja Robots in a force field that was sapping all their power. Dewey opened his mouth to call Mom, but then one of the Ninja-bots used his Sword of Fate to cut his way out of the force field in a shower of sparks. That was television as it should be. Dewey's mouth fell open and he settled down to watch.

Thanks to me and Reese, Dewey was back on track. That's what family's for.